Mark Sperring and Sarah Wa[rburton]

Daddy Lion's Tea Party

HarperCollins *Children's Books*

One bright, sunny day, Daddy Lion reached for his favourite teapot and smiled at the lion cubs.

"Today is the **PERFECT** day for a quiet little tea party," he announced.

But the three lion cubs looked doubtful...
They liked **BIG, NOISY** parties, not quiet little ones!

"Can we at least invite the chimps?" they asked.

Daddy Lion shook his mane.
"I don't think so," he said.
"Those chimps are
ALWAYS
monkeying about!"

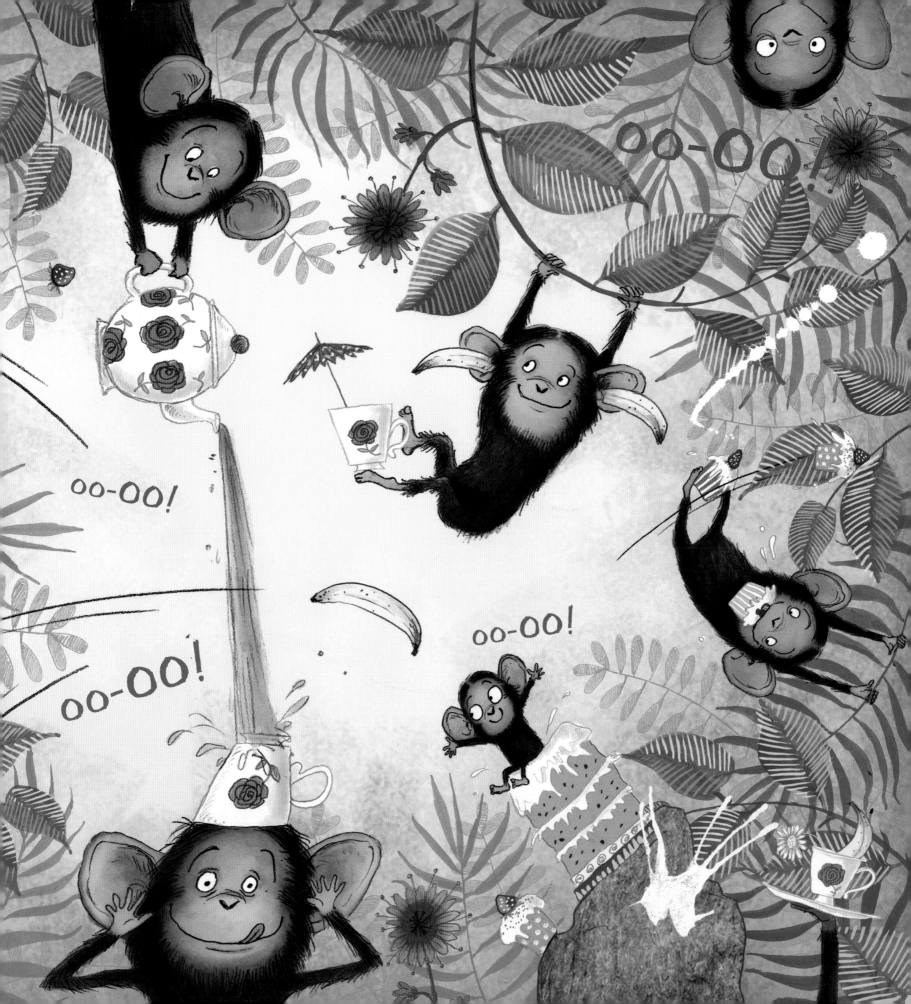

"Then how about the pot-bellied pigs and Rhino?" asked the cubs.
"Can they come, PLEASE and pretty PLEEEASE!?"

OINK

"Not today," said Daddy Lion. "The pot-bellied pigs always HOG the cream buns...

...and Rhino never stops charging about."

"Then what about all our other friends,"
asked the cubs, "can they come instead?"

"Well, my dears," sighed Daddy Lion,
"they could... **But** you know how
all the other animals *normally* behave...

Crocodile **SNAPS** at everyone...

SNAP!

Sloth only turns up when all the other guests have gone...

WHERE'S the PARTY?

and as for Skunk,

that **awful** Skunk...

So it was decided it would just be **Daddy Lion** and the lion cubs at the tea party.

Wouldn't that be nice?

There was just one

HUGE

problem...

Elephant (who was all ears) had overheard the

whole thing!

"Pssst... "

he whispered.

"Did you know?
Daddy Lion is having
a tea party and none
of us are invited!"

But Ostrich (for obvious reasons)
was only
half
listening...

So when she shook
the sand from her ears...

...she told the parrots (who were all talk)...

...what she **thought**
she'd heard Elephant say...

...which is how the parrots
ended up flying high
overhead, squawking...

"Daddy Lion is having a Tea Party

and We're ALL invited!!!"

And which is why...
just as Daddy Lion lifted his
favourite china tea cup daintily
to his lips, the lion cubs let out a

MIGHTY

cheer...

For there stood **ALL** the animals
ready to join in the fun.

"Well," said Daddy Lion,
"now you're here you might as
well all sit down, but remember,
this is a **quiet** little tea party, so,

best
behaviour,
please."

So down they sat, as nicely and politely
as they possibly could and no one
hogged the buns or monkeyed about.

But, just when the lion
cubs thought things were
a little too quiet, Ostrich
nudged Daddy Lion...

"Pssst," she said. "Look, everyone is staring at us!"

And for a moment *everyone froze...*

"Zoo Visitors..." muttered Daddy Lion.

"I think we should all ignore them...
and just behave as we **normally** would."

Which is how Daddy Lion's party finally turned into a...

RIP-ROARING, POOH-PONG-STINKING, BIG, NOISY, WILD SUCCESS...

And that is why, the very next day,
the lion cubs asked, "Can we PLEEEASE
have another *'quiet little tea party'*,
just like yesterday?!"

For Judith, Helen and James for
throwing the BEST tea parties! – M.S.

For Lee (our Daddy Lion), and all
the broken peaceful moments – S.W.

First published in paperback in Great Britain by HarperCollins Children's Books in 2015

1 3 5 7 9 10 8 6 4 2

ISBN: 978-0-00-748184-2

HarperCollins Children's Books is a division of HarperCollins Publishers Ltd.

Text copyright © Mark Sperring 2015
Illustrations copyright © Sarah Warburton 2015

Visit our website at: www.harpercollins.co.uk

Printed in China